PICTUREPEDIA

NOTE TO PARENTS

This book is part of PICTUREPEDIA, a completely
new kind of information series for children.
Its unique combination of pictures and words
encourages children to use their eyes to discover and
explore the world, while introducing them to a wealth
of basic knowledge. Clear, straightforward text
explains each picture thoroughly and provides
additional information about the topic.

'Looking it up' becomes an easy task with
PICTUREPEDIA, an ideal first reference for all types of
schoolwork. Because PICTUREPEDIA is also entertaining,
children will enjoy reading its words and looking
at its pictures over and over again. You can encourage
and stimulate further inquiry by helping your child
pose simple questions for the whole family to
'look up' and answer together.

D   JRS

D.K.

Dinosaurs.

560

DK

DORLING KINDERSLEY

LONDON, NEW YORK, AUCKLAND
DELHI, MUNICH, SYDNEY

DK www.dk.com

First published in Great Britain in 1993
by Dorling Kindersley Limited, London

This updated edition published in 2000 by:

Dorling Kindersley Limited
9 Henrietta Street, London WC2E 8PS, Great Britain

Dorling Kindersley Publishing Pty Limited
(A.C.N. 078 414 445)
118-120 Pacific Highway, St Leonards NSW 2065, Australia

Dorling Kindersley (India) Pvt. Ltd.
102/3 Kaushalya Park, Hauz Khas, New Delhi 110016, India

A CIP catalogue record for this
book is available from the British Library.

ISBN 0 7513 6911 X

Reproduction by Colourscan, Singapore
Printed and bound by L. Rex Printing Company Limited, China

DINOSAURS

A DORLING KINDERSLEY BOOK

CONTENTS

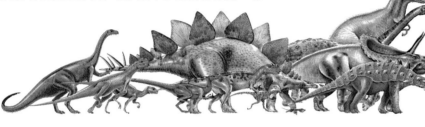

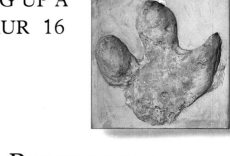

WHAT WERE THE DINOSAURS?

Stegosaurus

The only dinosaur you will ever see is a dead dinosaur! No human being has ever seen a real, live dinosaur, because the last of these incredible creatures died out about 65 million years ago, long before the first humans appeared. Huge dinosaur skeletons and life-like models can help us imagine what these fantastic animals were like. Dinosaurs were the biggest land animals of all time, and different to anything alive today.

Dinosaur Lookalike
Some of our best dinosaur lookalikes are reptiles. Dinosaurs were also reptiles. Unlike fish, reptiles lay eggs with shells. Reptiles are not like birds, because their skin is covered with bony scales. These scales also make them different to furry mammals.

Triceratops the Typical
Triceratops had a lot in common with many other dinosaurs. With sharp, deadly horns on its massive head, this dinosaur was a frightening sight!

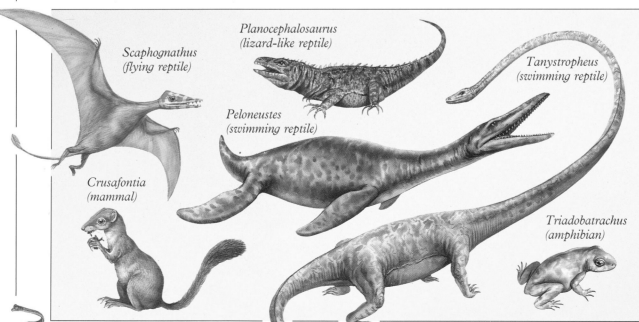

Scaphognathus (flying reptile)

Planocephalosaurus (lizard-like reptile)

Tanystropheus (swimming reptile)

Peloneustes (swimming reptile)

Crusafontia (mammal)

Triadobatrachus (amphibian)

Dinosaur-Free Zone
These creatures lived at the same time as the dinosaurs, but none of them were dinosaurs. No dinosaur swam in the seas or swooped through the skies, so swimming and flying reptiles were not dinosaurs. On land, reptiles, frogs and mammals spent their days hiding from the dinosaurs.

Brachiosaurus

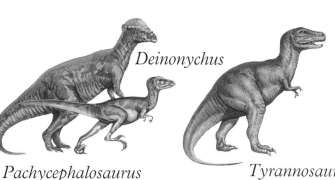

Deinonychus

Pachycephalosaurus

Tyrannosaurus

Dinosaur Assortment
Dinosaurs walked the Earth
for about 150 million years.
A huge variety of dinosaurs
lived during this time. So far,
about 600 different species
have been discovered.

*Triceratops had
tough, scaly skin,
like all dinosaurs.*

*Sharp horns and a
strong, bony neck frill
protected Triceratops
against attack.*

*Triceratops was 9 metres
long. Many dinosaurs
were this big, or
even bigger.*

*Legs as strong as pillars
were tucked underneath
Triceratops' bulky body.
All dinosaurs had a
similar way of standing.*

Stand Up Straight!
There is an important
difference between
living reptiles and
the dinosaurs.
Unlike today's
reptiles, dinosaurs
stood up straight!

*A dinosaur's
legs were tucked
underneath its
body, holding up
its bulky weight.*

*A lizard sprawls
along, with its
legs jutting out at
an awkward angle
from its body.*

DIFFERENT DINOSAURS

Dinosaurs were first named nearly 200 years ago. There has been an explosion of excitement about them ever since. The huge number of different dinosaur species makes the study of dinosaurs fascinating for everyone. Thousands of bones belonging to hundreds of different dinosaurs have now been discovered. Today, dinosaurs are big business, with millions of dinosaur books and toys on sale in the shops.

First and Last

Herrerasaurus was one of the first dinosaurs. It lived about 230 million years ago. *Tyrannosaurus* was one of the last dinosaurs and became extinct about 65 million years ago. Today, we are closer in time to *Tyrannosaurus*, than *Tyrannosaurus* was to *Herrerasaurus*!

Dinosaur Ancestor

Scientists think that over millions of years, all the different dinosaurs may have developed from one single reptile, called *Marasuchus*. The hips and long legs of this primitive reptile are similar to those of the earliest dinosaurs.

Classic Jurassic

The middle part of the dinosaur age is called the Jurassic Period. It started about 200 million years ago and lasted for 60 million years.

The Age of the Dinosaurs

Dinosaurs didn't all live at the same time. When one species died out, another rose up to take its place. The dinosaur age is split into the Triassic, Jurassic and Cretaceous Periods. The first dinosaurs appeared during the Triassic Period, about 230 million years ago.

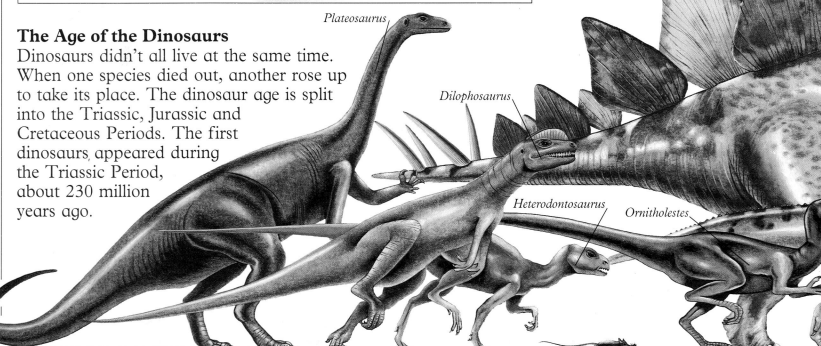

Plateosaurus

Dilophosaurus

Heterodontosaurus

Ornitholestes

Handy Hips
Looking at the hip bones of dinosaurs helps us split the dinosaurs into two main groups. If the hip bones are arranged like a bird's, the dinosaur is in the 'bird-hipped' group. If the hip bones are arranged like a lizard's, the dinosaur is in the 'lizard-hipped' group.

Bird Hips
Iguanodon was in the bird-hipped group, with *Triceratops*, *Euoplocephalus*, and *Stegosaurus*.

Stegosaurus

Euoplocephalus

Iguanodon

Triceratops

Lizard Hips
The lizard-hipped group includes two-legged meat-eaters, like *Tyrannosaurus rex*. Plant-eating sauropods, like *Diplodocus*, were also lizard-hipped.

Diplodocus

Tyrannosaurus rex

Cretaceous Creatures
The last stage in dinosaur history is called the Cretaceous Period. This stage lasted for about 75 million years. The fiercest ever meat-eaters lived during this time, alongside their heavily armoured prey.

Stegosaurus

Ceratosaurus

Compsognathus

Tyrannosaurus rex

Saltasaurus

Torosaurus

Euoplocephalus

LANDS OF THE DINOSAURS

Jungles are hot and steamy places, crammed with lush plants. Today, there are only a few areas of jungle left, but during the dinosaur age, most of the world had a tropical climate, like a jungle. Fossils of palm trees and other tropical plants have been found south of London, England. This proves that the climate and landscape were very different there about 100 million years ago!

Becoming a Fossil

Fossils are the remains of things that lived long ago. Very few living things become fossils. Trillions of dinosaurs lived and died without trace, but only a few thousand dinosaur fossils have been found. *Baryonyx* was a very lucky find!

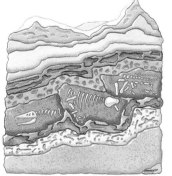

4. Over time, wind and rain wore the rock away. The fossils broke through the surface of the rock.

3. Over millions of years, movements deep down in the Earth forced the bones upwards, and broke up the skeleton's shape.

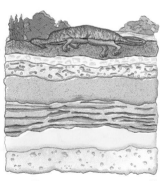

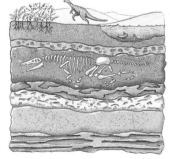

2. *Baryonyx* was slowly buried under many layers of mud and sand. In time, these layers turned to rock, and minerals filled the spaces in the bones.

1. *Baryonyx* was alive in the early Cretaceous Period. When it died, a layer of sand and mud quickly covered its body.

Finding *Baryonyx*

In 1983, a new dinosaur was dug out of this clay pit in southern England. The dinosaur was named *Baryonyx*. Fossils of plants, insects and fish were also found at the Cretaceous fossil site.

Living Fossil

Dragonflies often settled on plants by the waterside. Some dragonfly fossils are very well preserved, and show how little dragonflies have changed in their long history.

The Fisher King

Baryonyx was a big dinosaur, with a long, narrow head a bit like a crocodile's. About 110 razor-sharp teeth lined its snappy jaws. *Baryonyx* probably lived near water, and scooped fish up from the water with its long claws. We know it ate fish, because fossils of fish scales were found inside its ribcage.

This claw was the first Baryonyx fossil to be found.

Leaf Print

The leaf that made this fossil once grew on a flowering plant. Flowers first appeared during the Cretaceous Period, when *Baryonyx* was still alive and fishing by the water's edge.

Pond Life

Pond life was rife in the days of *Baryonyx*. Snails may be slow, but this one has survived for millions of years as a fossil! Snails have not changed very much over their long history.

Fish may have made up Baryonyx's last meal.

11

DISCOVERY!

Dinosaur bones were dug out of the Earth long before people knew what kind of creatures they belonged to. Huge, mysterious bones were first found in China over 2,000 years ago. We now believe these bones belonged to dinosaurs, but at the time of discovery, people thought they belonged to dragons! The name 'dinosaur' is quite new. It was invented in 1842 by a Victorian fossil hunter called Richard Owen. He used it to describe this family of ancient reptiles. Dinosaur means 'terrible reptile'.

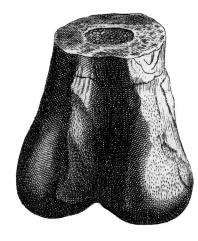

Baffling Bone
This bone baffled everyone when it was discovered in England in 1677. Some thought it belonged to a giant human! Scientists today know it was part of the thigh bone of the big dinosaur *Megalosaurus*.

Megalosaurus **Model Maker**
In 1853, Richard Owen designed a life-sized model of *Megalosaurus*, which is still on display in London. It is very interesting to see what people over a century ago thought dinosaurs looked like. Our modern view is very different.

Naming *Megalosaurus*
Megalosaurus was the first dinosaur to be named and described in detail. William Buckland was an English fossil hunter. He found a jaw bone like this in 1824, and named its owner *Megalosaurus*. This means 'big reptile'.

Megalosaurus was very large and lived on land. The model gets this right.

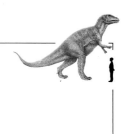

Walk Tall

Megalosaurus' hip bones were arranged like the hip bones of a modern lizard. This means *Megalosaurus* was one of the 'lizard-hipped' dinosaurs. The discovery of its hips also proved that *Megalosaurus* walked upright on two legs, and didn't crawl on all fours as in Owen's model.

Ilium

Pubis

Femur

Ischium

Modern *Megalosaurus*

Since the days of Owen and Buckland, *Megalosaurus* has had a big change of image. *Megalosaurus* was an active, fierce meat-eater. Its powerful jaws and bulky body helped it to attack and kill the huge plant-eaters of its day, like *Diplodocus*.

Megalosaurus was three metres tall when it reared up on its back legs.

Owen's model looks like a cross between a lizard and an elephant!

Huge, powerful back legs meant that Megalosaurus could charge quickly after its prey.

Getting this close to Megalosaurus in real life would have been very dangerous!

Strong legs take the weight of Megalosaurus' body. Owen was right about the way dinosaurs stood upright.

DINOSAURS AROUND THE WORLD

Skeletons of dinosaurs have been found all over the world, in Europe, America, Africa, Asia and Australia. Today, these continents are separated by the sea. If you want to see all the dinosaur fossil sites, you have to cross the sea to get to them. During the dinosaur age, all the continents were joined together. Dinosaurs could easily move around the world.

Euro Dino
Many skeletons of *Plateosaurus* have been found all over central Europe. *Plateosaurus* lived in the Triassic Period.

All American
When the horns of *Triceratops* were first discovered in America, it was thought they belonged to a bison! *Triceratops* lived in the Cretaceous Period.

Triassic

Jurassic

Cretaceous

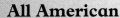

Barosaurus

Brachiosaurus

The Dinosaur Age
The beginning of the dinosaur age is called the Triassic Period. All the continents were joined in one mass of land. The middle of the dinosaur age is called the Jurassic Period. During this time, the land mass split into two parts. The end of the dinosaur age is called the Cretaceous Period. In this period, the continents drifted farther apart, leaving dinosaurs stranded in different parts of the world.

Changing Places
Barosaurus and *Brachiosaurus* fossils have been found as far apart as Africa and North America! Scientists believe today's continents were once joined together as one huge area of land, because there is no other way these dinosaurs could get from one continent to the other.

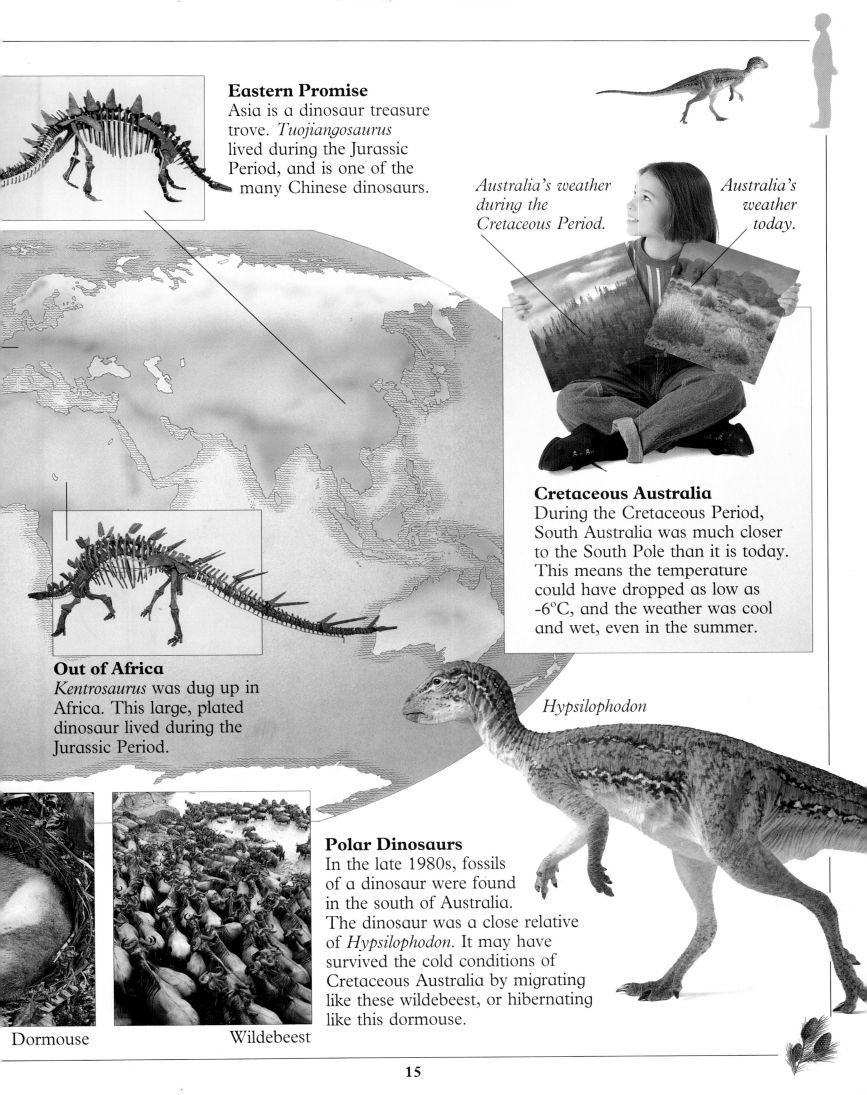

Eastern Promise
Asia is a dinosaur treasure trove. *Tuojiangosaurus* lived during the Jurassic Period, and is one of the many Chinese dinosaurs.

Australia's weather during the Cretaceous Period.

Australia's weather today.

Cretaceous Australia
During the Cretaceous Period, South Australia was much closer to the South Pole than it is today. This means the temperature could have dropped as low as -6°C, and the weather was cool and wet, even in the summer.

Out of Africa
Kentrosaurus was dug up in Africa. This large, plated dinosaur lived during the Jurassic Period.

Hypsilophodon

Polar Dinosaurs
In the late 1980s, fossils of a dinosaur were found in the south of Australia. The dinosaur was a close relative of *Hypsilophodon*. It may have survived the cold conditions of Cretaceous Australia by migrating like these wildebeest, or hibernating like this dormouse.

Dormouse

Wildebeest

15

DIGGING UP A DINOSAUR

Dinosaur fossils are very rare, because they are only found buried in certain types of rock. Dinosaurs became extinct at the end of the Cretaceous Period, so any rock that formed after this time does not contain any dinosaur fossils. Rocks at the bottom of the sea are usually free of dinosaur fossils, because dinosaurs lived on land. The best places to hunt for dinosaur bones are in rock layers that formed at the bottom of swamps, lakes or rivers.

This skeleton has been very well preserved. Most of the skeleton is still buried under the ground.

The rock around the fossil has been slowly and carefully chipped away.

Drawing fossils is an important job on a dinosaur dig.

This Tyrannosaurus skeleton is 12 metres long. It is lying curled up on its left side.

Old Bones, New Technology

Modern technology, like this ground-penetrating radar, can be used to find bones below the rock surface. In the 1980s, a dinosaur named *Seismosaurus* was found in this way, in New Mexico.

Dinosaur Trap

The Dinosaur National Monument in America is one of the world's richest dinosaur treasure troves. It was once a sandy riverbed, which trapped many dying dinosaurs and preserved their bones.

Handle with Care

Although dinosaurs were strong when they were alive, their fossils are very fragile now. Digging up a dinosaur is a slow and very delicate process.

1. The thick layers of rock above the dinosaur are often cleared away with mechanical diggers, and sometimes blasted away with explosives.

2. The last 20 centimetres or so of rock above the dinosaur are removed very carefully with tools.

3. The exact positions of the bones are then mapped out and recorded with drawings and photographs.

Fossil Collection

Dinosaur bones are not the only kind of fossils found at dinosaur sites.

Footprints   Skin   Stomach stones

Eggs   Droppings   Teeth

4. The fragile bones must be covered with plaster for protection, before they can be moved away from the site.

5. At last, the strengthened bones are loaded up in a van and driven to a laboratory for further study.

REBUILDING A DINOSAUR

Thick bones in the neck held up the heavy weight of Tyrannosaurus' head.

Jigsaws can be tricky, especially if some pieces are missing and pieces from different jigsaws are mixed in. People who rebuild dinosaur skeletons are faced with a similar puzzle. Fossil bones must be put together in the right order to form a skeleton. Bones belonging to different dinosaurs may have found their way into the collection by mistake. Missing bones are modelled by looking at the bones of similar dinosaurs. Broken bones must be cleaned and mended before they can be assembled.

Back at the Lab

Dinosaur bones are taken from the fossil site to a laboratory. Experts clean and mend them, ready for rebuilding into a skeleton. Sometimes, fossils may be prepared for study only, rather than for display.

Belly Ache

Early this century, scientists argued over how to rebuild the skeleton of *Diplodocus*. Some believed *Diplodocus* was built like a lizard, with long legs sprawling out from its body. This was an impossible pose. *Diplodocus* would have needed to drag its belly through a trench to walk!

1. First, hard protective plaster must be removed from the bone with special tools.

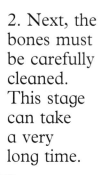

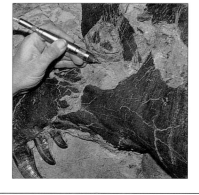

2. Next, the bones must be carefully cleaned. This stage can take a very long time.

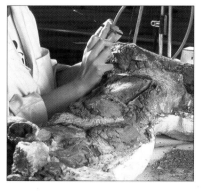

3. The bones are then treated with resin to make them stronger. They must also be repaired if necessary.

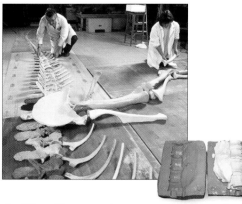

4. Finally, copies are made of the bones using a light material, like fibre glass. The copies, called casts, can be put together to make a museum display.

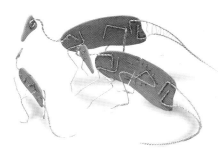

Super Skull
Some fossils are almost perfectly preserved. After millions of years buried under rock, this *Tyrannosaurus* skull did not need much patching up in the fossil laboratory!

Model Making
This model of a *Maiasaura* nest was sculpted by a scientific artist.

1. The basic *Maiasaura* shapes are made up with wood and wire.

Building *Tyrannosaurus*
This skeleton of *Tyrannosaurus rex* has been on display in an American museum since 1915. Today, scientists think that a big mistake was made in the way the skeleton was put up. They now think *Tyrannosaurus* held its tail up high above the ground.

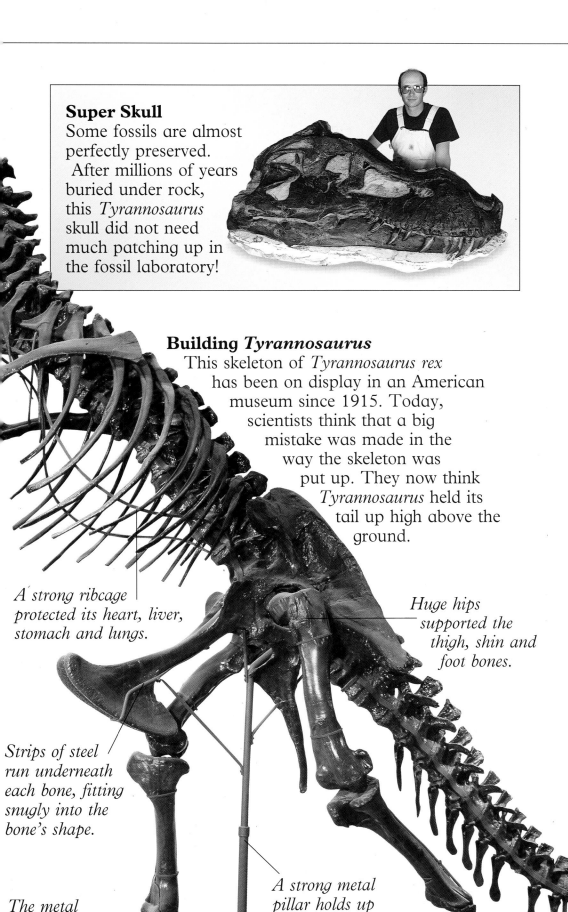

A strong ribcage protected its heart, liver, stomach and lungs.

Huge hips supported the thigh, shin and foot bones.

Strips of steel run underneath each bone, fitting snugly into the bone's shape.

The metal framework supporting the skeleton is called an armature.

A strong metal pillar holds up the metal strips, supporting the full weight of the skeleton.

2. The nest site is built up around the models. The wire skeletons are covered with paper and clay.

3. The clay models are carefully painted a sandy colour. In life, *Maiasaura* was probably well camouflaged.

The tail bones were an extension of Tyrannosaurus' spine.

19

LOOKING CLOSER

Staring up at the towering skeletons of dinosaurs can make you feel tiny. But bones alone do not give the whole picture of a living, breathing dinosaur. What colour was the dinosaur when it was alive? How strong were its muscles, and how big were its heart and lungs? Looking closely at animals alive today gives us useful clues about features, such as the skin colour of dinosaurs. We can even imagine what their insides may have looked like!

Weight Watcher
Barosaurus was a very heavy sauropod, like *Brachiosaurus*. Both dinosaurs had hollow bones in their spines. This was a useful weight-saving device.

Brachiosaurus' heart nestled underneath its lungs. It must have had very high blood pressure for the heart to be able to pump blood all around its body.

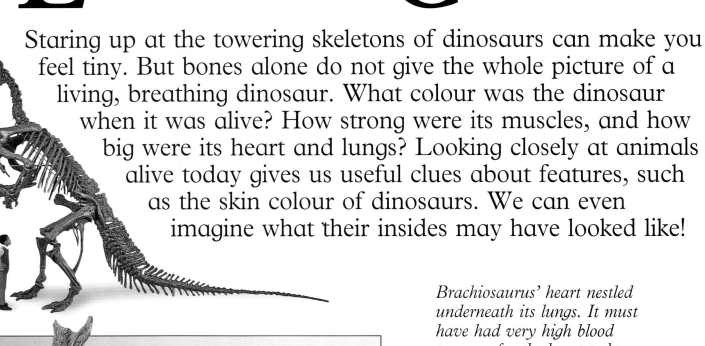

Brachiosaurus finished digesting its food in the longest part of its gut, called the small intestine.

Two massive lungs fitted snugly inside its ribcage.

Tough food was broken down inside the thick walls of the stomach.

Moisture was taken out of digested plants in this part of the intestine.

Powerful tail muscles made it possible to swing this bulky tail.

Sturdy leg bones supported the 77-tonne bulk of Brachiosaurus.

Strong neck muscles held up its long neck.

Brachiosaurus had nostrils on top of its head.

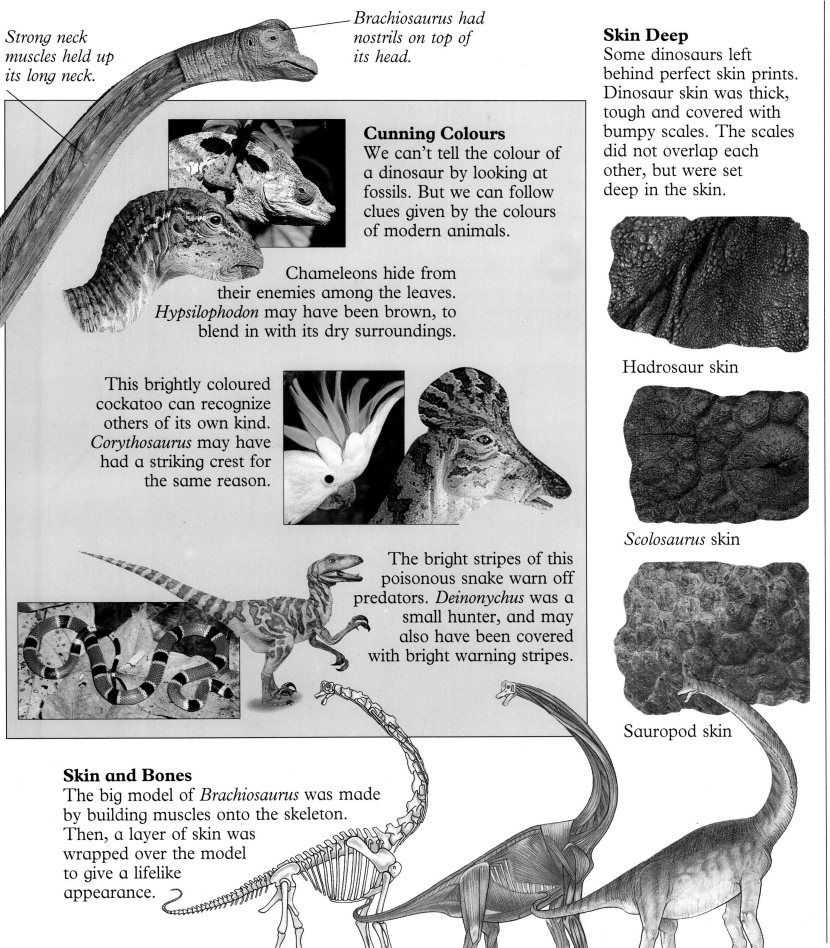

Skin Deep
Some dinosaurs left behind perfect skin prints. Dinosaur skin was thick, tough and covered with bumpy scales. The scales did not overlap each other, but were set deep in the skin.

Hadrosaur skin

Scolosaurus skin

Sauropod skin

Cunning Colours
We can't tell the colour of a dinosaur by looking at fossils. But we can follow clues given by the colours of modern animals.

Chameleons hide from their enemies among the leaves. *Hypsilophodon* may have been brown, to blend in with its dry surroundings.

This brightly coloured cockatoo can recognize others of its own kind. *Corythosaurus* may have had a striking crest for the same reason.

The bright stripes of this poisonous snake warn off predators. *Deinonychus* was a small hunter, and may also have been covered with bright warning stripes.

Skin and Bones
The big model of *Brachiosaurus* was made by building muscles onto the skeleton. Then, a layer of skin was wrapped over the model to give a lifelike appearance.

BIG VEGETARIANS

Plant-eating dinosaurs were some of the biggest animals that ever roamed the Earth. Imagine stepping into the footprint of a *Barosaurus* – it would be big enough to have a bath in! The big vegetarian dinosaurs were sauropods, a name which means 'reptile foot'. These peaceful creatures grew to huge sizes on a diet of plants alone.

Gentle Giants
Sauropods had small heads, bulky bodies and long necks and tails.

Brachiosaurus

Camarasaurus

A long tail could come in useful for whacking an enemy, but most of the time it was used to help Barosaurus balance.

Teeth

Stones

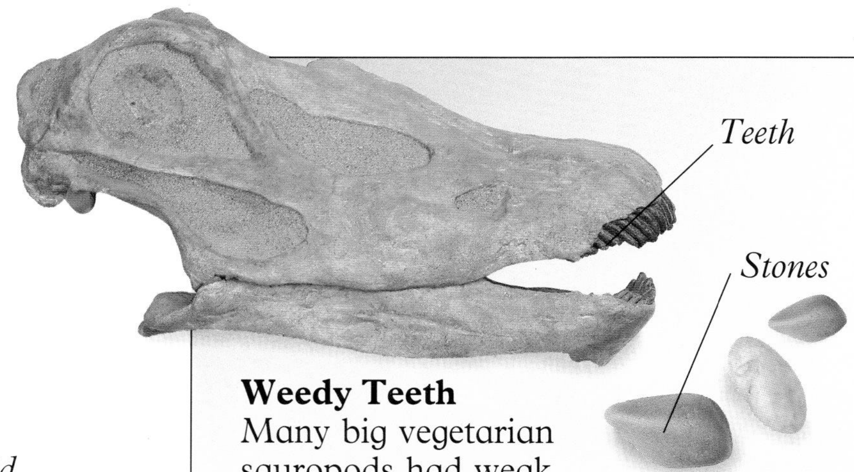

Weedy Teeth
Many big vegetarian sauropods had weak teeth. This meant they did not chew plants, but often swallowed them whole. Gulping down stones may have helped grind up food in their stomachs. These stones, called gastroliths, churned tough plants into a pulp.

Mamenchisaurus

Apatosaurus

Its feet were flat and padded, just like an elephant's.

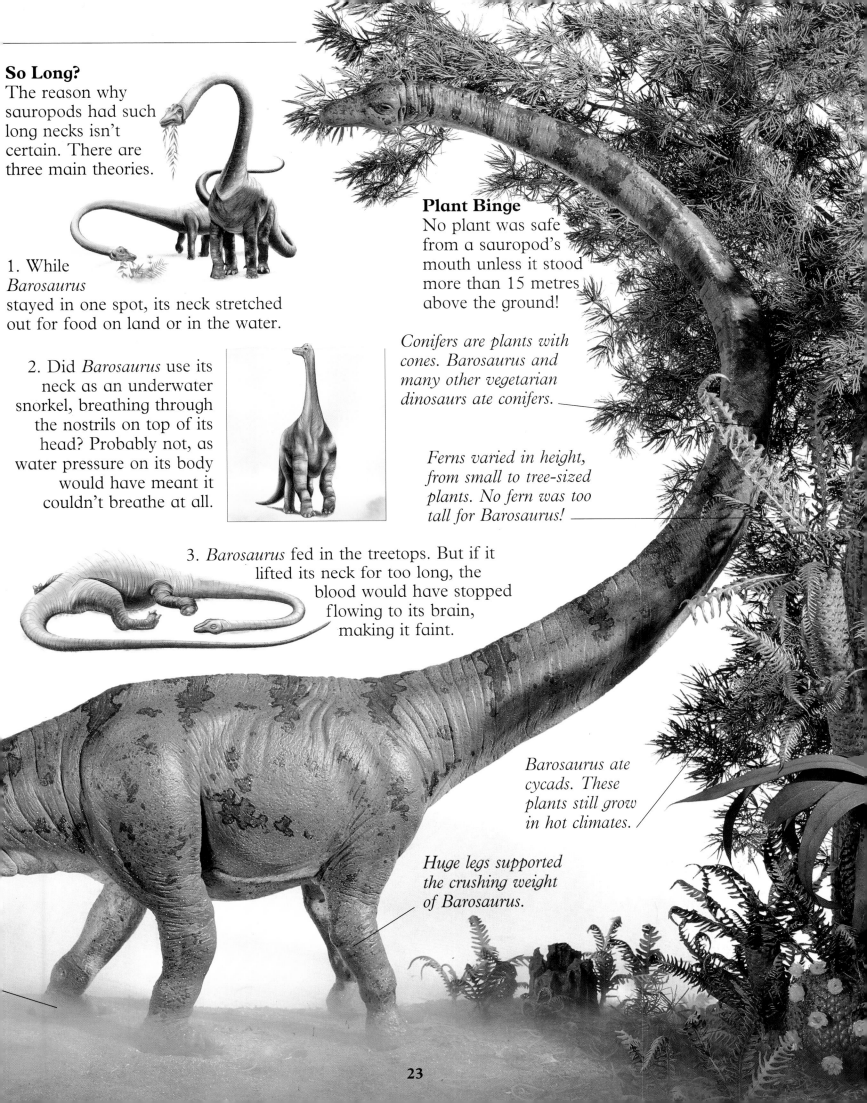

So Long?

The reason why sauropods had such long necks isn't certain. There are three main theories.

1. While *Barosaurus* stayed in one spot, its neck stretched out for food on land or in the water.

2. Did *Barosaurus* use its neck as an underwater snorkel, breathing through the nostrils on top of its head? Probably not, as water pressure on its body would have meant it couldn't breathe at all.

3. *Barosaurus* fed in the treetops. But if it lifted its neck for too long, the blood would have stopped flowing to its brain, making it faint.

Plant Binge

No plant was safe from a sauropod's mouth unless it stood more than 15 metres above the ground!

Conifers are plants with cones. Barosaurus and many other vegetarian dinosaurs ate conifers.

Ferns varied in height, from small to tree-sized plants. No fern was too tall for Barosaurus!

Barosaurus ate cycads. These plants still grow in hot climates.

Huge legs supported the crushing weight of Barosaurus.

FEEDING ON PLANTS

Nearly all the huge treetop-munching dinosaurs died by the end of the Jurassic Period, about 140 million years ago. The very tall plants disappeared with them. Smaller dinosaurs then arrived on the scene. *Iguanodon* was well adapted to chewing and chomping. Its jaws were packed with rows of ridged teeth. These grinders pounded away at leaves *Iguanodon* nipped off with a sharp, beaky snout.

Chewy Chops
Your cheeks keep food inside your mouth as you chew. Unlike the big sauropods, *Iguanodon* had cheeks to hold in plant food while it chewed with its teeth.

Big, fleshy cheeks kept food in Iguanodon's mouth as it ate.

A sharp beak nipped off the leaves, and strong teeth at the back of its mouth chewed them into a pulp.

Iguanodon ate plants, but no meat, like all the bird-hipped dinosaurs.

Iguanodon browsed on ferns and horsetails.

Snatch a Snack
Iguanodon had a sharp thumb claw, which may have ripped down tough leaves. A bendy finger grasped plants tightly.

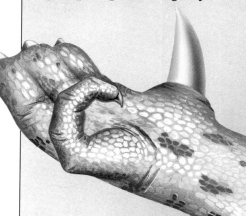

Vegetarian Mouths

The mouths of these dinosaurs were well adapted for eating plants. *Heterodontosaurus* had three types of teeth, for cutting, puncturing and grinding. *Edmontosaurus* had a broad snout for gathering up big leafy mouthfuls. *Hypsilophodon* had a bony beak, with short teeth farther back in its mouth for chopping up its food.

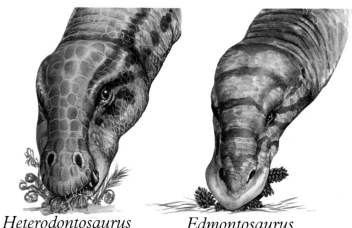

Heterodontosaurus   *Edmontosaurus*   *Hypsilophodon*

Jaw bone of *Edmontosaurus*

Rows of teeth for grinding down plants

Captain Beaky

Just like a turtle, *Iguanodon* had a beak, which it used for nipping plants. This horny beak never stopped growing, but was ground down by a constant diet of tough leaves. Behind the beak was a solid set of teeth, grinding up and down and from side to side.

Fighting Back

Dinosaurs were the biggest plant-eaters of all time. Plants had to find ways of fighting back to survive. Some were so successful, they outlived the dinosaurs, and are still around.

The spikes of a monkey puzzle tree put off most dinosaurs. Today, no animal will touch them.

Battle of the Flowers

The first flowering plants bloomed about 100 million years ago. They were successful because they could spread their seeds and reproduce more quickly than plant-eaters could gobble them up.

Waxy pine needles taste as bad today as they did in the dinosaur age.

HUNTING IN PACKS

Not all dinosaurs were plant-eaters. Packs of hungry meat-eating dinosaurs roamed all over the land, looking for their next meal. *Deinonychus* was a small dinosaur that hunted in a pack. It could outrun its prey and pounce to the kill with frightening accuracy. Dinosaurs much bigger than *Deinonychus* lived in fear of this clever hunter. *Deinonychus* was named after its most deadly weapon – its name means 'terrible claw'.

Running Reptiles
Deinonychus was in a family of meat-eating dinosaurs called the dromaeosaurids, which means 'running reptiles'.

Compsognathus

Compsognathus fossil

Bavarisaurus

Velociraptor

Lizard Lunch
Many pack-hunting dinosaurs chased other dinosaurs, but the smaller hunters enjoyed a diet of lizards or shrew-like mammals. This fossil of the hen-sized *Compsognathus* has the bones of its last meal – a *Bavarisaurus* lizard – inside its stomach.

The body of Deinonychus was light and speedy. This was ideal for chasing after prey.

Dromaeosaurus

Deadly Claw
Deinonychus had a claw on the tip of each of its toes, but one claw was much bigger than the rest. This huge, sharp talon could swipe round in a semi-circle, slashing a deadly wound into the flesh of the dinosaur's prey.

The claw was 13 centimetres long.

Troodon

Brain Box

Each member of a pack of hunting dinosaurs had to time its movements and communicate with the rest of the group. *Deinonychus* had a big skull, which held a large brain, shown here in red. This means that *Deinonychus* would have been intelligent enough to hunt in a pack.

Why Hunt in Packs?

One wolf cannot attack a deer on its own, but a pack of wolves can easily pull one down. The reason for hunting in packs is the same now as it was at the time of the dinosaurs. Small, meat-eating dinosaurs joined together to overpower much bigger dinosaurs.

Sharp eyesight was very useful for spotting prey.

Sharp, jagged teeth pointed backwards, for a strong, tearing bite.

Often just a quarter of the size of its prey, Deinonychus was about 3 metres long and 1.8 metres tall.

This plant-eating Tenontosaurus bled to death from the gashes made by the Deinonychus pack.

ENORMOUS MEAT-EATERS

Like tigers today, *Tyrannosaurus rex* may have hunted alone, terrorizing its prey with surprise attacks. This fierce dinosaur was a carnivore, which means it lived on a diet of meat. One of the biggest meat-eaters ever to walk on this planet, it was heavier than an elephant and as tall as a two-storey building. Its name means 'king of the tyrant reptiles'.

Hunters need good eyesight and a strong sense of smell. Large parts of Tyrannosaurus' brain controlled its senses of sight and smell.

Tyrannosaurus had a massive skull. It took the shock of crashing into prey at speeds of up to 32 kilometres per hour.

Tyrannosaurus may have charged with open jaws, ready to sink its deadly teeth into its prey. Big chunks of flesh were swallowed whole.

Its short 'arms' weren't long enough to reach its mouth, but they may have been used to grip and kill prey.

Duck-Billed Dinner
Tyrannosaurus probably hunted duck-billed dinosaurs, called hadrosaurs. It may have hidden among the trees, waiting for the right moment to charge at a peaceful herd of grazing duckbills.

Life-Sized Tooth

A *Tyrannosaurus* tooth grew up to 18 centimetres long.

A Tyrannosaurus tooth was covered with tough enamel.

The sharp edge of the tooth was serrated, like a kitchen knife.

Look how small a human tooth is!

Meet the Family

The big meat-eating dinosaurs belong to the carnosaur group. This name means 'flesh lizard'.

Stretch Those Legs

Tyrannosaurus' short 'arms' may also have been used to help the dinosaur up after a rest on the ground.

1. Small front arms hold its body steady, as *Tyrannosaurus* begins to move.

2. *Tyrannosaurus* then lifts its head and body backwards, stretching out its long back legs.

3. *Tyrannosaurus* stands up straight. The weight of its tail balances its big head.

Cannibal Dinosaurs

A cannibal is a living thing that eats its own kind. Some meat-eating dinosaurs may have been cannibals. This skeleton of a dinosaur called *Coelophysis* was found with the tiny bones of a baby *Coelophysis* inside its stomach.

lbertosaurus

Tarbosaurus

Dilophosaurus

Ceratosaurus

Allosaurus

SURVIVAL

Hunting wasn't always easy for meat-eaters like *Tyrannosaurus rex*. As the big carnivores developed sharper teeth and more powerful jaws, their prey developed better ways of defending themselves. Some species probably sat tight throughout an attack, secure under heavy armour. Other dinosaurs had more active ways of defending themselves, from lashing out with their spiky tails to swinging their bone-splintering tail clubs.

Under Cover
When in danger from attack, *Hylaeosaurus* may have hidden under its heavy armour of spikes.

Fossil Weapon
This fossil belonged to a dinosaur called *Ankylosaurus*. The ankylosaurids were a group of dinosaurs that were experts at self-defence. Each member of this group had a club of solid bone on the tip of its tail.

Built Like a Tank
Euoplocephalus was an ankylosaurid. It was the size of a tank and was also built like one. An armour of tightly fitting bone plates hugged its bulky body.

Death Club
Euoplocephalus had a very nasty tail club. Direct hits spelled danger and even death for a predator like *Tyrannosaurus*. A broken leg from such a blow meant this fierce meat-eater couldn't move to defend itself from other tyrannosaurids.

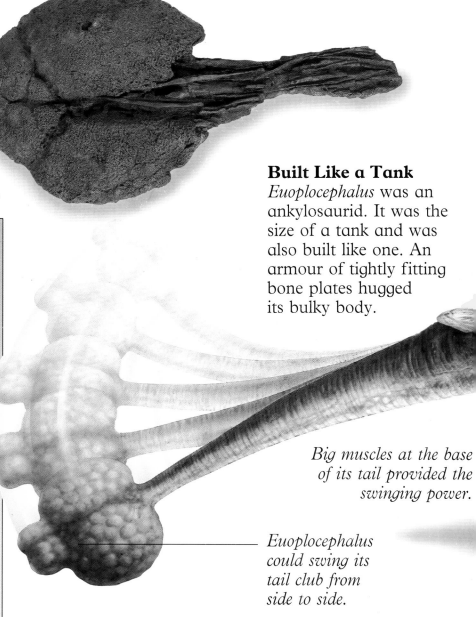

Big muscles at the base of its tail provided the swinging power.

Euoplocephalus could swing its tail club from side to side.

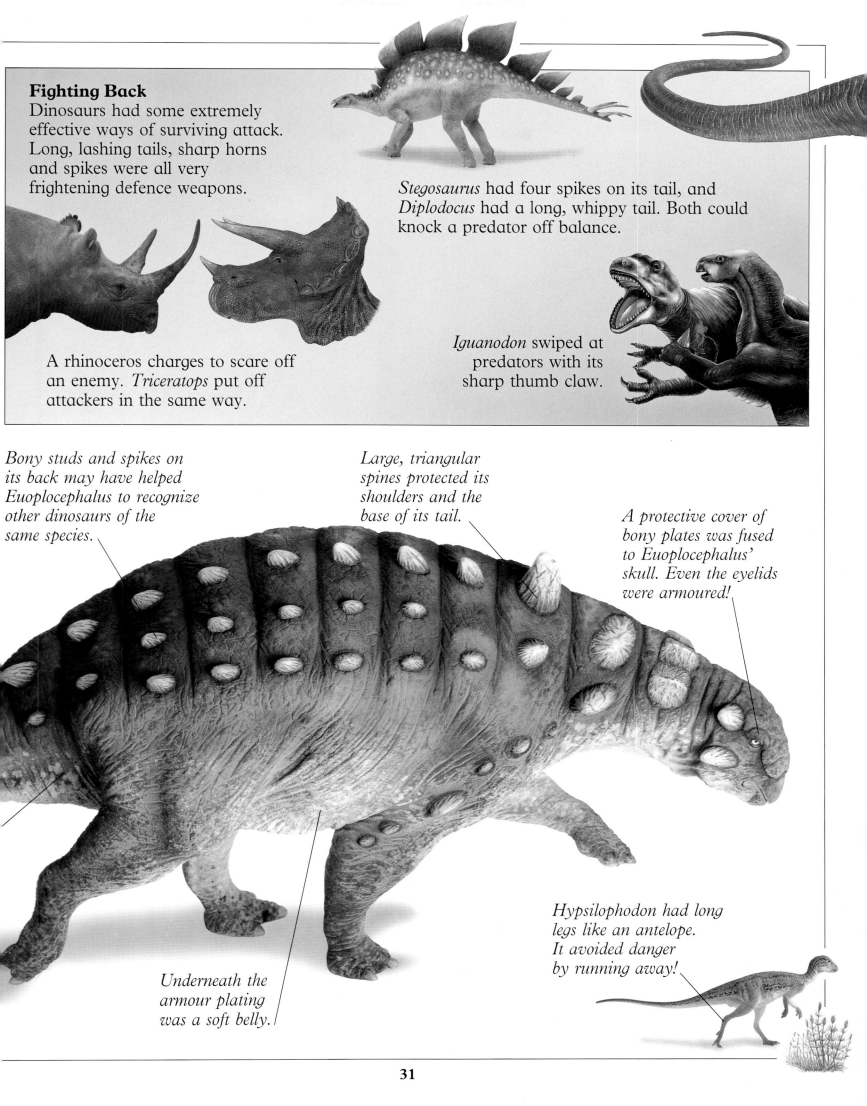

Fighting Back

Dinosaurs had some extremely effective ways of surviving attack. Long, lashing tails, sharp horns and spikes were all very frightening defence weapons.

Stegosaurus had four spikes on its tail, and *Diplodocus* had a long, whippy tail. Both could knock a predator off balance.

A rhinoceros charges to scare off an enemy. *Triceratops* put off attackers in the same way.

Iguanodon swiped at predators with its sharp thumb claw.

Bony studs and spikes on its back may have helped Euoplocephalus to recognize other dinosaurs of the same species.

Large, triangular spines protected its shoulders and the base of its tail.

A protective cover of bony plates was fused to Euoplocephalus' skull. Even the eyelids were armoured!

Hypsilophodon had long legs like an antelope. It avoided danger by running away!

Underneath the armour plating was a soft belly.

BRAIN POWER

Dinosaurs are often thought of as slow, clumsy and above all, stupid. It is true that some had tiny brains – *Stegosaurus'* brain was no bigger than a walnut and was as light as a hen's egg. But not all the dinosaurs were as dim as *Stegosaurus*. Many smaller hunters, like *Troodon*, had large brains in relation to their body size. This meant they had some intelligence.

Troodon's head was 30 centimetres long. It held a big brain.

The eyes of Troodon faced forwards. It had sharp eyesight.

Troodon was only 2.4 metres long. This small meat-eater was fast and clever enough to hunt in packs.

Battle of the Brains
Troodon was one of the most intelligent dinosaurs. Its brain was big compared to the size of its body. *Stegosaurus* was not quite so smart. Its brain was tiny compared to the huge size of its body.

A Very Modern Dinosaur
Using small, intelligent dinosaurs such as *Troodon* as a basis, some scientists have tried to work out what would have happened to them if they had not become extinct. Their surprising conclusion is that, after another 65 million years, *Troodon* might well have evolved to look a bit like a human.

Nut Case

Brains are made of soft tissue and rot away when an animal dies. To work out the size of *Stegosaurus'* brain, we must look at the hole in its skull where its brain would have been. Here, its brain is coloured red.

If dinosaurs were still around, they would not win many intelligence tests. Today's mammals and birds have more brain power than any dinosaur.

From its snout to the tip of its tail, Stegosaurus was 6 metres long and weighed 2 tonnes.

Stegosaurus had a tiny head compared to its body. It was only about 40 centimetres long.

1. Modern mammals are top of the class.

2. Birds are the second most intelligent group.

A nerve centre at the base of the tail acted like a 'second brain'. It controlled the movements of the tail.

Bundle of Nerves

There is a hollow in the area of bone just above *Stegosaurus'* hips. The space may have held a mass of nerves, which operated its tail and back legs. *Stegosaurus* could do no thinking with this bigger 'second brain'.

3. Dinosaurs were less intelligent than birds are today.

Spinal cord

Brain inside skull

'Second brain'

4. Modern reptiles are as clever as most dinosaurs.

LIVING IN A GROUP

Corythosaurus Crest

Corythosaurus had a hollow crest on the top of its head. It breathed in air through its nostrils. The air then passed into the tubes in its crest, and continued on into the windpipe.

Animals often live in family groups, because they need safety in numbers from predators. This was certainly true of the duck-billed dinosaurs. Herds of crested duckbills must have been particularly noisy, as their strange crests were probably used as hooters to communicate with the rest of the group. We know that some dinosaurs lived in herds, because large groups of their fossil bones and footprints have been found together.

Each dinosaur communicated with the herd by honking with its crest.

Group Behaviour

Pachycephalosaurus means 'thick-headed lizard'. Unlike the crest of *Corythosaurus*, the dome on top of this dinosaur's head was not hollow, but made of solid bone. *Pachycephalosaurs* lived in herds, and males may have fought head-butting contests to win a mate.

Down the Mine

In 1878, 39 *Iguanodon* skeletons were found close together in a mine in Belgium. Because so many *Iguanodon* died in the same place, scientists believe they lived in a herd. The skeletons are displayed in a Belgian museum.

Crazy Crests

People used to think that some duckbill crests were used for air storage, or for head protection as the dinosaur ran through the forests. It is more likely that the crests made honking noises, to help each species recognize its own kind.

Lambeosaurus

Parasaurolophus

Saurolophus

A keen sense of smell gave good warning of predators prowling in the distance.

Good eyesight and keen hearing meant that each member of the herd was alert to danger.

Calling All Duckbills . . .

Inside *Parasaurolophus*' crest was a maze of air passages. Just as you can blow into a trombone to make a blast of sound, *Parasaurolophus* could have made loud hooting noises to the rest of the herd by snorting air through the tubes in its crest.

Corythosaurus had long back legs, and could sprint away if the herd was attacked.

FAMILY LIFE

Dinosaurs laid eggs, just like reptiles do today. In 1978, the remains of a dinosaur nesting site were found in America. Many egg fossils were found, with adults and young nearby. The dinosaur was named *Maiasaura*, which means 'good mother reptile'. Clues left behind suggest that *Maiasaura* lived in family groups and that the adults looked after their young very carefully.

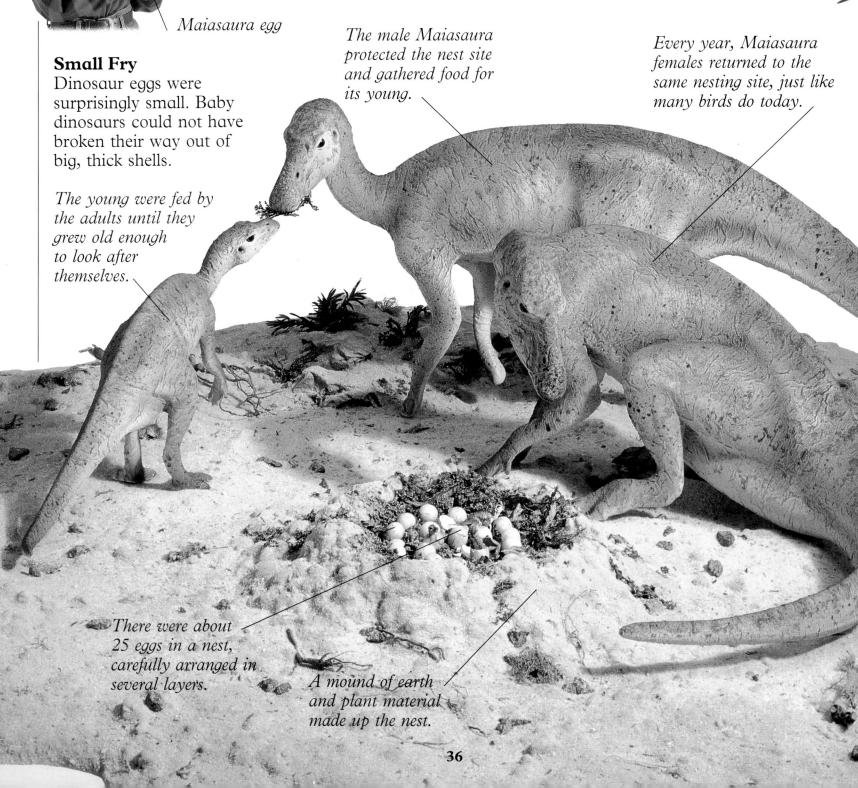

Maiasaura egg

Small Fry
Dinosaur eggs were surprisingly small. Baby dinosaurs could not have broken their way out of big, thick shells.

The young were fed by the adults until they grew old enough to look after themselves.

The male Maiasaura protected the nest site and gathered food for its young.

Every year, Maiasaura females returned to the same nesting site, just like many birds do today.

There were about 25 eggs in a nest, carefully arranged in several layers.

A mound of earth and plant material made up the nest.

Stop Thief!

Some dinosaurs may have turned to a life of crime, stealing eggs from unattended nests. *Oviraptor* had three strong fingers on each hand, which it might have used to grip eggs. A tough, toothless beak could then crack open an egg. This greedy dinosaur's name means 'egg thief'.

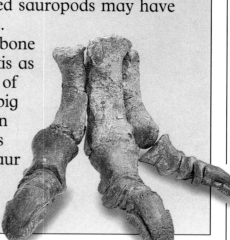

Eggs in a Maiasaura nest may have taken up to three months to hatch.

Tiny, helpless Maiasaura hatchlings probably stayed in the nest and were fed by the adults.

Spaced Out

Large groups of *Maiasaura* probably nested together, to protect themselves from attack. The nests found in Montana were spaced about 7 metres apart. Each mother had enough room to sit on her nest to keep the eggs warm.

Maiasaura nests

Growing Up

Baby dinosaurs grew very quickly to reach full size. The texture of duckbill bones gives us clues about the speed of their growth – a baby probably grew to adult size in just a few years.

An adult Maiasaura was about 9 metres long, from snout to tail.

At the age of one, it was only a metre long.

Hatchlings were about 50 cm long.

Maiasaura started life inside an egg.

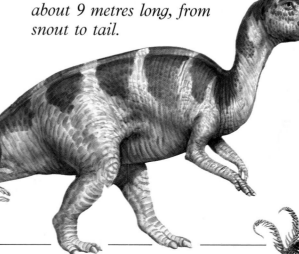

MONSTERS AND MIDGETS

Brachiosaurus

Some dinosaurs were very big, but not all of them were giants. Small, bird-like dinosaurs shared the prehistoric landscape with the most enormous creatures ever to walk the Earth. One of the smallest dinosaurs, *Compsognathus*, weighed no more than a hen. This is 50,000 times lighter than *Brachiosaurus*, one of the heaviest known dinosaurs. *Brachiosaurus* was so tall that he could have looked right over the top of a three-storey building!

African elephant

Ten Times Table
Life on Earth today is a scaled-down version of life in the world of the dinosaurs. The biggest creature to walk on land today is the African elephant. The largest dinosaur was about ten times bigger than this!

Active *Allosaurus*?
Allosaurus was the biggest meat-eater at the end of the Jurassic Period. It may have hunted in packs. But some people think it was too big and clumsy to chase after prey. Perhaps it fed on animals that had already died.

This life-sized model shows that it is just as well no human ever lived at the time of the dinosaurs!

Big Bones
This fossil of a shoulder blade belonged to the dinosaur '*Supersaurus*', a relative of *Brachiosaurus*. This giant was nearly three times taller than a giraffe.

Big Heads

The last of the bird-hipped dinosaurs, the ceratopians, lived during the final 20 million years of the dinosaurs. These horned dinosaurs gradually developed bigger heads, longer horns and taller neck frills. *Triceratops* was a giant compared to its tiny ancestors.

Bagaceratops   *Protoceratops*   *Centrosaurus*   *Triceratops*

Small is Beautiful

Compsognathus was one of the smallest known dinosaurs. This tiny meat-eater was only 70 centimetres long.

Its small jaws were packed with spiky teeth. Compsognathus means 'pretty jaw'.

Tiny claws on its fingers acted like sharp pincers.

Compsognathus' stiff tail helped it to balance as it ran along.

Monster Munch

A warm-blooded animal has to eat lots of food to keep up its body temperature. A cold-blooded animal doesn't need as much food, and is not always active when the air is cold. Scientists argue whether dinosaurs were warm- or cold-blooded. If dinosaurs were warm-blooded, they would have had impossibly huge appetites.

Long legs meant it was built for lightning speed.

Small Beginnings

When the fierce dinosaurs prowled the Earth, tiny shrew-like mammals cowered behind trees and rocks. Larger mammals did not evolve until the dinosaurs had died out.

A warm-blooded Ceratosaurus would have eaten this much meat in a year.

This is all the meat a cold-blooded Ceratosaurus would have needed in a year.

DINOSAUR ATHLETICS

A small dinosaur called *Hypsilophodon* was once thought to have spent its days perched up in trees. This was because the bones in its foot had been put together in the wrong way. There are many more misunderstandings about dinosaurs. Perhaps the most common is that they were all slow and blundering. The truth is that many were very athletic. Some, like the graceful *Gallimimus*, could run as fast as a racehorse!

Road Runner
Some dinosaurs were very similar to birds. *Gallimimus* could sprint along at fast speeds, just like an ostrich can today.

When Gallimimus ran, it stretched out its tail like a stiff rod. This was good for balance.

Long, strong fingers were good for grappling and grasping.

The hip bones were arranged like the hip bones of a modern bird. This helped Gallimimus to run fast.

Gallimimus had long, thin hind legs. It could run at speeds of up to 56 kilometres per hour.

From beak to tail, Gallimimus was about four metres long.

Gallimimus had no teeth in its beak. It probably ate things that were easy to swallow, like fruit, small animals, and even other dinosaurs' eggs.

Water Workout
In 1944, some fossil footprints were found in Texas, America. The prints had been made by the two front feet of a sauropod. Such a big dinosaur could not balance on its front feet. Some scientists think it may have been floating in water as it propelled itself forwards, steering with its back legs.

Full Speed Ahead
Triceratops could have charged faster than a rhinoceros does today, at speeds of up to 40 kilometres per hour. Its flexible joints, big leg bones and huge calf muscles powered it along.

Leg of a *Triceratops*

Strong bones took the pounding stress of a fast run.

Flexible bone joints helped Triceratops move quickly and easily.

Huge calf muscles provided the power for galloping.

Speed Check
A dinosaur's speed can be worked out by measuring the gap between its footprints. This gap and the length of the dinosaur's leg are calculated together to give its speed. No dinosaur ran at top speed all the time, so the speed worked out from a set of footprints is probably not the dinosaur's personal best.

SEA SWIMMERS

During the dinosaur age, the world's climate was warmer than today. There were no icecaps, and there was much more water in the sea. The swelling seas were full of some very strange living things. No dinosaur lived in the sea, but the oceans were brimming with many other reptiles. Giant reptiles like *Pliosaurus* were some of the most frightening predators ever to swim in the sea.

Good eyesight was important for seeing through the murky seawater.

Water Baby

Ichthyosaurs were so well adapted to life in the sea that they didn't need to drag themselves onto land to lay eggs. They gave birth to live young in the water. This ichthyosaur died as she was giving birth. The fossil shows the baby coming out, tail first.

Rows of sharp teeth crunched the hardest of bones.

Baby Whales

Whales give birth under water, just like ichthyosaurs did, millions of years ago.

Triassic Swimmers

During the dinosaur age, there were four main groups of swimming reptiles. The placodonts and nothosaurs of the Triassic Period were not very well adapted to life in the open seas. Placodonts never swam beyond the shallow coastal waters, and nothosaurs probably spent much of their time resting on land.

Placodus was 2 metres long. It was a placodont.

Nothosaurus was a nothosaur. It was 3 metres long.

Pistosaurus was the first plesiosaur. It was 3 metres long.

Jurassic and Cretaceous Swimmers

The swimming reptiles of the Jurassic and Cretaceous Periods were much better adapted to sea life. Plesiosaurs flapped their flippers to 'fly' under water. Ichthyosaurs were the best swimmers. They moved gracefully through the water with their streamlined bodies.

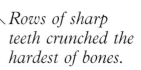

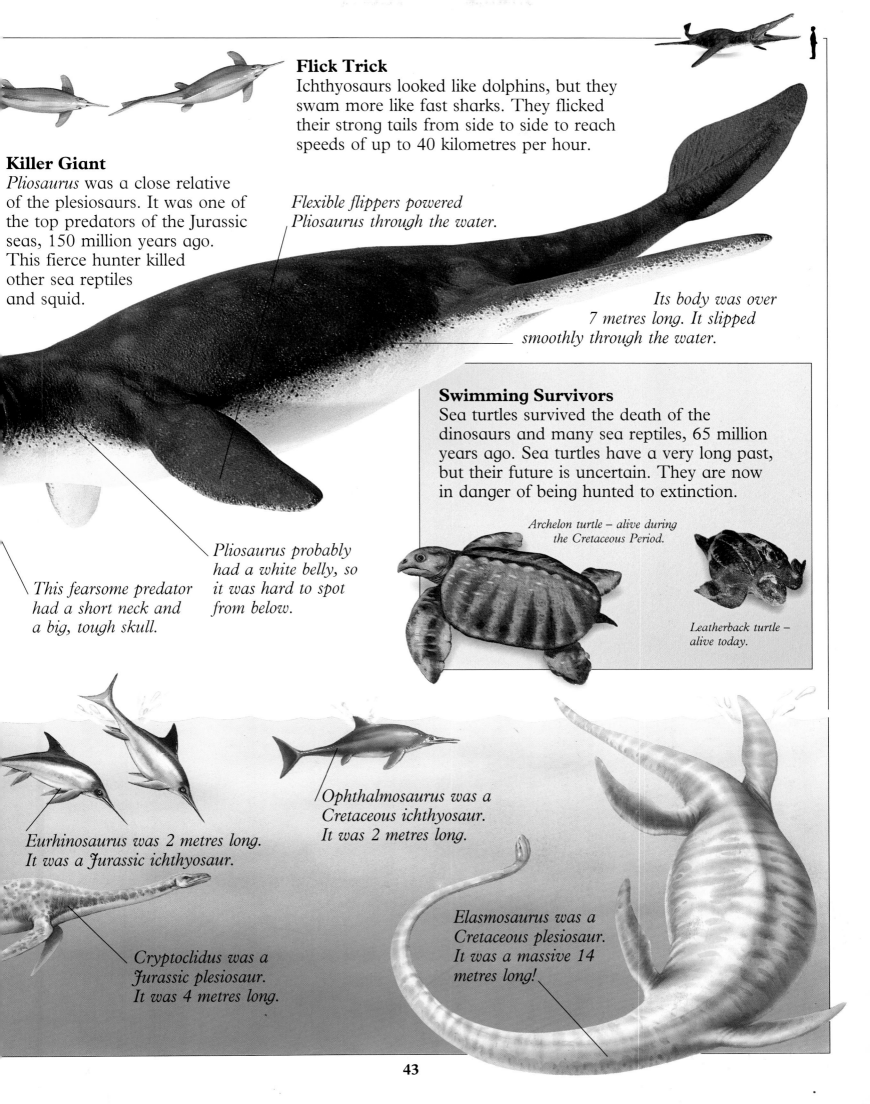

Flick Trick

Ichthyosaurs looked like dolphins, but they swam more like fast sharks. They flicked their strong tails from side to side to reach speeds of up to 40 kilometres per hour.

Killer Giant

Pliosaurus was a close relative of the plesiosaurs. It was one of the top predators of the Jurassic seas, 150 million years ago. This fierce hunter killed other sea reptiles and squid.

Flexible flippers powered Pliosaurus through the water.

Its body was over 7 metres long. It slipped smoothly through the water.

Swimming Survivors

Sea turtles survived the death of the dinosaurs and many sea reptiles, 65 million years ago. Sea turtles have a very long past, but their future is uncertain. They are now in danger of being hunted to extinction.

Archelon turtle – alive during the Cretaceous Period.

Leatherback turtle – alive today.

This fearsome predator had a short neck and a big, tough skull.

Pliosaurus probably had a white belly, so it was hard to spot from below.

Ophthalmosaurus was a Cretaceous ichthyosaur. It was 2 metres long.

Eurhinosaurus was 2 metres long. It was a Jurassic ichthyosaur.

Cryptoclidus was a Jurassic plesiosaur. It was 4 metres long.

Elasmosaurus was a Cretaceous plesiosaur. It was a massive 14 metres long!

FLYING REPTILES

When herds of dinosaurs were roaming about on land, the skies were crowded with the flapping wings of flying creatures. These fliers, called pterosaurs, were not dinosaurs, but a closely related group of reptiles. All pterosaurs could fly or glide. Their large wings were covered with leathery skin, like bats. They also had long necks, big heads and toothy beaks.

Big Flapper

Pteranodon was a pterosaur with a seven-metre wingspan. It soared above the sea with slow flaps of its big wings. Once in full flight, *Pteranodon* could rest its wings, gliding silently on hot air currents.

1. Strong muscles held its wings high above its body.

2. One big flap, and the wings swept downwards.

3. Pteranodon glided away on warm currents of air.

Dimorphodon probably cracked tough fish bones with its big, strong beak.

Magnificent Flying Machine

Quetzalcoatlus was the biggest flying animal that ever lived. When this fantastic flier stretched its wings, they measured about 14 metres across. Look how many children are needed to equal its whacking wingspan!

Sharp, pointed teeth were quite widely spaced inside the roomy beak.

Food for Flight

Pterosaurs flew over rivers, lakes and oceans, scooping up fish. Some may have snapped up low-flying insects, too.

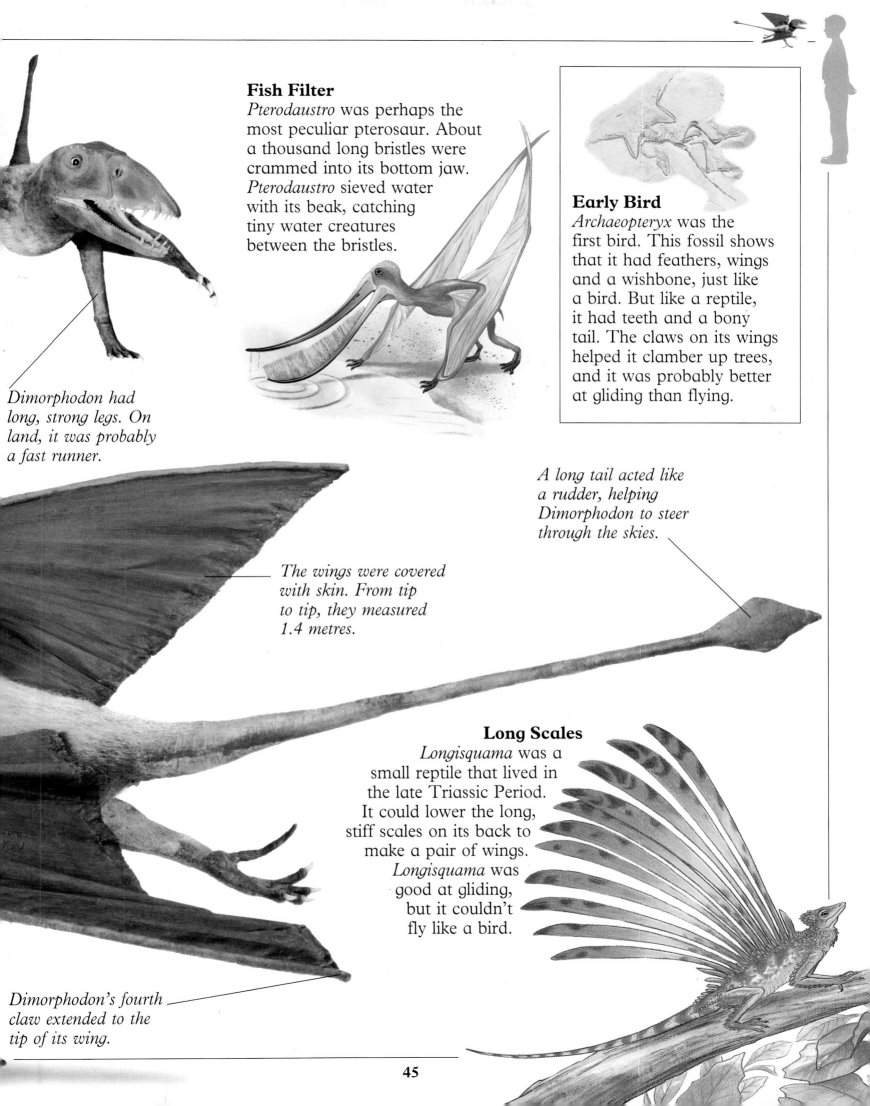

Fish Filter

Pterodaustro was perhaps the most peculiar pterosaur. About a thousand long bristles were crammed into its bottom jaw. *Pterodaustro* sieved water with its beak, catching tiny water creatures between the bristles.

Dimorphodon had long, strong legs. On land, it was probably a fast runner.

Early Bird

Archaeopteryx was the first bird. This fossil shows that it had feathers, wings and a wishbone, just like a bird. But like a reptile, it had teeth and a bony tail. The claws on its wings helped it clamber up trees, and it was probably better at gliding than flying.

A long tail acted like a rudder, helping Dimorphodon to steer through the skies.

The wings were covered with skin. From tip to tip, they measured 1.4 metres.

Long Scales

Longisquama was a small reptile that lived in the late Triassic Period. It could lower the long, stiff scales on its back to make a pair of wings. *Longisquama* was good at gliding, but it couldn't fly like a bird.

Dimorphodon's fourth claw extended to the tip of its wing.

DEATH OF THE DINOSAURS

Rock Solid Proof
The rock on the Earth's surface is formed in layers. The deeper the layer, the older the rock. No dinosaur fossil has been found above the layer that formed 65 million years ago. This proves the last dinosaurs died this long ago.

We can tell how old dinosaur fossils are by looking at the age of the rock they were found in. From this, we know that the last of the dinosaurs died out about 65 million years ago. But we can only guess why this happened. Perhaps a huge disaster wiped out all the dinosaurs in one go, or they may have become extinct over a very long time.

From Outer Space
Some scientists believe that a huge asteroid crashed into the Earth at the end of the Cretaceous Period. Possible evidence for this has been found in Central America, in Yucatán. The huge impact of the asteroid could have spelled doom for the dinosaurs.

North America

South America

Yucatán

The asteroid may have hurtled towards Earth at about 241,350 kilometres per hour.

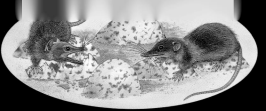

Slow Change

Dinosaurs may not have disappeared overnight. The world's climate could have cooled over millions of years, slowly killing off the dinosaurs. New plants grew in this colder climate. The warm jungles that covered most of the dinosaurs' world slowly turned into cooler forests.

Wild Guesses

Many theories try to explain the death of the dinosaurs. Some are more unlikely than others! Perhaps peckish mammals ate their eggs.

Or perhaps the dinosaurs were poisoned by new, nasty plants. But no single theory can explain what really happened.

The Survivors

Life on Earth did not end with the death of the dinosaurs. Birds, mammals, reptiles and amphibians are some of the animal groups that survived, and are still around today.

Bird

Mammal

Reptile

Amphibian

What a Hole

Scientists now think an asteroid hit Earth at the end of the Cretaceous Period, making a crater in Yucatán that was 180 kilometres wide. This photo shows a similar crater that was made by an asteroid in Arizona.

Shocked quartz

Iridium

Finding Proof

The asteroid crushed rock in the Earth's surface as it hit Yucatán. Shocked quartz has been found at the crater site. Iridium is a rare metal, found in asteroids. There are high levels of iridium in the rock that contains the last dinosaur fossils.

The disaster would have set off a chain reaction. 400 million, million tonnes of rock and dust blocked out the Sun's light and the temperature dropped to -10°C. Acid rain fell on the dinosaurs.

GLOSSARY

Asteroid A rock or metal object that orbits the Sun like a planet.

Bird-hipped Bird-hipped dinosaurs had hips rather like birds. The dinosaurs in this group were vegetarians.

Carnivore An animal that eats the flesh of another animal.

Carnosaur A big meat-eating theropod.

Cold-blooded Animals which depend on the Sun's heat to keep their body temperature level are 'cold-blooded'.

Conifer A tree with cones, for example a pine or fir.

Cretaceous The last period of the dinosaur age. It started about 140 million years ago, and ended about 65 million years ago.

Cycad A stumpy plant similar to a palm tree, which was very common during the dinosaur age.

Dinosaur A reptile that lived on land and walked with legs tucked underneath its body. The dinosaurs appeared in the Triassic Period. The last dinosaurs disappeared at the end of the Cretaceous Period.

Evolve All living things evolve over time. They change very slowly over a series of generations, to adapt to their environment.

Extinction The death of a whole group, or species, of animals.

Fossil The preserved remains of something that was once alive.

Gastrolith A stone swallowed to pound up food inside a dinosaur's stomach.

Hibernation Some animals fall into a deep sleep during the cold winter months to save energy. This is called hibernation.

Ichthyosaur A swimming reptile, very well adapted to life at sea.

Iridium A rare chemical element, found in meteorites and in the core of the Earth.

Jurassic The middle period of the dinosaur age. It started about 200 million years ago and ended about 140 million years ago.

Lizard-hipped Lizard-hipped dinosaurs had hips rather like those of modern lizards. The group included vegetarians and meat-eaters. It was one of the two main dinosaur groups.

Mammal Mammals are warm-blooded. They breathe air and feed their babies on milk. During the dinosaur age, all mammals were very small.

Migration The regular movement of animals from one place to another to find food or escape cold weather.

Placodont A turtle-like reptile of the Triassic seas.

Plesiosaur A sea reptile that used flippers to swim.

Pterosaur A flying reptile that lived at the same time as the dinosaurs, but was not a dinosaur.

Reptile A cold-blooded, egg-laying animal, covered with scales. Some prehistoric reptiles may have been warm-blooded, like the flying pterosaurs.

Sauropod Long-necked and long-tailed giant of the Jurassic and Cretaceous Periods.

Theropod A meat-eating, lizard-hipped dinosaur. Most theropods stood upright on two legs.

Triassic The first part of the dinosaur age. It lasted from about 245 to 200 million years ago. The first dinosaurs evolved during the Triassic Period.

Warm-blooded Animals that can control their body temperature inside their bodies, without depending on the Sun for constant heat, are warm-blooded.

Acknowledgements

Photography: Peter Chadwick, Andy Crawford, John Downes, Lynton Gardiner, Colin Keates, The Colour Company, Tim Kelly, Gary Kevin, Chris King, Dave King, Cyril Laubscher, Kevin Mallett, Ray Moller, Tim Ridley, Dave Rudkin, Karl Shone, Harry Taylor and Andreas Von Einsiedel.

Illustration: Roby Braun, Jim Channell, Roy Flooks, Linden Artists, Alan Male, Richard Manning, Jane Pickering, Simon Roulstone and John Temperton.

Models: Roby Braun; Crystal Palace Park, London; Donks Models; Graham High/Centaur Studios: Brachiosaurus, Iguanodon, Triceratops; John Holmes; Jeremy Hunt/Centaur Studios: Barosaurus, Baryonyx, Corythosaurus; Norrie Carr Model Agency; Reconstruction of Dimorphodon by Arril Johnson for Bristol City Museums & Art Gallery; Scallywags Model Agency.

Picture Credits

Ancient Art & Architecture Collection: 12cla; **Michael Benton:** 17clb, 18br; **Black Hills Institute of Geological Research:** Ed Gerken 18clb, 19tc; **Courtesy of Brigham Young University:** 38br; **Bruce Coleman Ltd:** Erwin & Peggy Bauer 21tc, Eric Crichton 24bl, 25bl, Gerald Cubitt 43cr, M.P.L. Fogden 21bl, Jeff Foott Productions 42c, endpapers, M.R. Phicton 17cra, John Shaw 47tl, Rod Williams 21cla, Joseph Van Wormer 30tl, 31tl; **Geoscience Features:** 47cl; **David Gillette PhD:** 17tl; **The Image Bank:** Gabriel M. Corian 17cla; **Museum of the Rockies:** Bruce Selyem 16br, 17cl, & bc, 37cr; **NASA:** 46cr; **NHPA:** Sorensen & Olsen 15c; **Natural History Museum, London:** back cover tl, 10bc, 12clb, tr & bc, 17cl & cb, 18cl, bc & crb, 21cra, 33tc, 37cra; **Oxford Scientific Films:** E.R Degginger / Animals Animals 6c, John Downer 15bl, Renee Lynn/Photo Researchers Inc.: 28cr, Tom McHugh 27tr, Owen Newman 14-5bc; **Planet Earth Pictures:** Georgette Douwman 25cl, Jonathan Scott 40cr; **Royal Belgian Institute of Natural Sciences, Brussels, Belgium:** 34bc; **Science Photo Library:** David A. Hardy 46bc, Prof. Erwin Mueller 47c, NASA 5br, 47bl, Dr. Robert Spicer 46cl, Erik Viktor 46bl; **Dr. Peter Wellnhofer:** 44cla; **Dr.R.Wild:** Staatliches Museum Für Naturkunde, Stuttgart 42clb; **Yale University, Peabody Museum:** J.H Ostrom 26br; **ZEFA:** D. Baglin 15cr.

tl – **top left**
cra – **centre right above**
clb – **centre left below**
br – **bottom right**
bc – **bottom centre**

tr – **top right**
cr – **centre right**
crb – **centre right below**
tc – **top centre**

cla – **centre left above**
cl – **centre left**
bl – **bottom left**
cb – **centre below**

INDEX

A

Africa **14, 15**
Albertosaurus **29**
Allosaurus **29, 38**
America **14**
ancestor **8, 39**
ankylosaurid **30**
Ankylosaurus **30**
Apatosaurus **22**
Archaeopteryx **45**
armour **30**
armature **19**
arthritis **37**
Asia **14, 15**
asteroid **46**
Australia **14, 15**

B

Bagaceratops **39**
Barosaurus **14, 20, 22-23**
Baryonyx **10-11**
Bavarisaurus **26**
beak **24, 25, 37, 41, 44**
bird **6, 33, 45**
bird-hipped **9, 24**
blood **20**
body temperature **39**
bone plates **30**
Brachiosaurus **14, 20-21, 22, 38**
brain **27, 28, 32-33**
Buckland, William **12**

C

Camarasaurus **22**
cannibal **29**
carnivore **30**
carnosaur **28**
Centrosaurus **39**
ceratopians **39**
Ceratosaurus **9, 29, 39**
China **12**
claw **26**
climate **10, 23, 47**
Coelophysis **29**
cold-blooded **39**
Compsognathus **9, 26, 38, 39**
conifer **23**
Corythosaurus **21, 34-35**
Cretaceous **8, 9, 10, 11, 14, 42, 43, 46**
Crusafontia **6**
Cryptoclidus **43**
cycad **23**

D

Deinonychus **7, 21, 26-27**
Dilophosaurus **8, 29**
Dimorphodon **44-45**
Diplodocus **9, 18, 31**
dragon **12**
dragonfly **10**
dromaeosaurid **26**
Dromaeosaurus **26**
duckbill **28, 34, 35, 37**

E

Edmontosaurus **25**
egg **6, 36, 41**
Elasmosaurus **43**
England **10**
Euoplocephalus **9, 30-31**
Eurhinosaurus **43**
extinction **43, 46, 47**

F

femur **13**
fern **23, 24**
fish **6, 10, 11, 44**
flowers **11, 25**
footprints **17, 41**
fossil **10, 11, 12, 14, 15,16, 17, 18, 19, 21, 30, 36, 42, 45, 46, 47**

G

Gallimimus **40-41**
gastroliths **22**

H

hadrosaur **21, 28**
hatchling **37**
heart **20**
Herrerasaurus **8**
Heterodontosaurus **8, 25**
hibernation **15**
horsetail **24**
Hylaeosaurus **30**
Hypsilophodon **15, 21, 25, 31, 40**

I

Ichthyosaurus **42, 43**
Iguanodon **9, 24, 31, 34, 37**
ilium **13**
iridium **47**
ischium **13**

J

jaws **11, 24, 25, 28, 30, 39**
jungle **10, 47**
Jurassic **8, 14, 24, 38, 42, 43**

K

Kentrosaurus **15**

L

Lagosuchus **8**
Lambeosaurus **35**
lizard **13**
lizard-hipped **9, 13**
Longisquama **45**
lungs **19, 20**

M

Maiasaura **19, 36-37**
Mamenchisaurus **22**
mammal **6, 33, 39**
Megalosaurus **12-13**
migration **15**
monkey puzzle tree **25**
muscles **20, 41, 44**

N

nesting site **19, 36, 37**
nothosaur **42**
Nothosaurus **42**

O

Ornitholestes **8**
Oviraptor **37**
Owen, Richard **12, 13**

P

Pachycephalosaurus **7, 34**
Parasaurolophus **35**
Peloneustes **6**
Pistosaurus **42**
placodont **42**
Placodus **42**
Planocephalosaurus **6**
Plateosaurus **8, 14**
plesiosaur **42, 43**
Pliosaurus **42-43**
predator **21, 31, 35, 42**
Protoceratops **39**
Pteranodon **44**
Pterodaustro **45**
pterosaur **44, 45**
pubis **13**

Q

Quetzalcoatlus **44**

R

reptile **6, 7, 8, 22, 28, 33, 42, 43, 44, 45**
ribcage **19, 20**

S

Saltasaurus **9**
Saurolophus **35**
sauropod **20, 21, 22, 23, 24, 37, 40**
scale **6**
Scaphognathus **6**
Scolosaurus **21**
shocked quartz **47**
skin **17, 21**
skull **27, 28, 31, 43**
small intestine **20**
snail **11**
South Pole **15**
spike **31**
spine **20, 31**
Stegosaurus **6, 9, 31, 32-33**
Stenonychosaurus **26, 32**
stomach **19, 20, 22, 29**
'Supersaurus' **38**

T

tail **20, 30, 31, 33**
tail club **30**
Tanystropheus **6**
Tarbosaurus **29**
teeth **22, 24, 25, 28, 29, 30, 44**
Tenontosaurus **27**
thumb claw **24, 31**
Triadobatrachus **6**
Triassic **8, 14, 42, 45**
Triceratops **6-7, 9, 14, 31, 39, 41**
Troodon **32**
Tuojiangosaurus **15**
turtle
  Archelon **43**
  Leatherback **43**
  Sea **43**
Tyrannosaurus rex **7, 8, 9, 28-29, 30**

V

vegetarian **22, 25**
Velociraptor **26**

W

warm-blooded **39**
windpipe **34**
wingspan **44**

Y

Yucatán **46, 47**